FLOWER FAIRIES
of the SUMMER
~ A ~
CELEBRATION

PLANTAIN AND MOON-DAISY DANCING TOGETHER,
ALL THROUGH THE BEAUTIFUL SUNSHINY WEATHER.

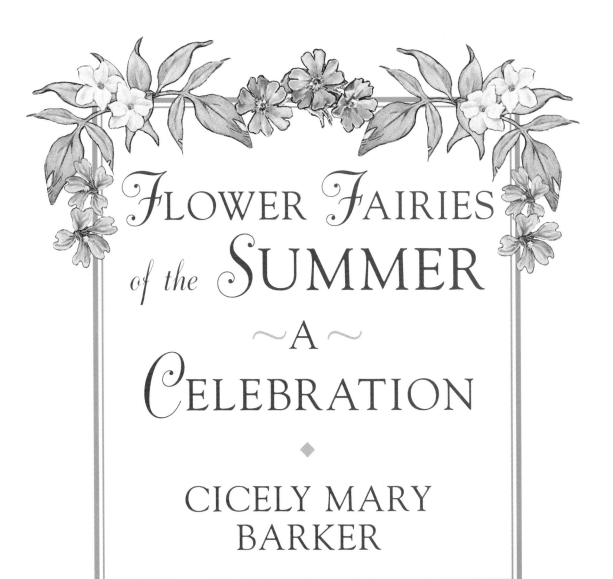

FLOWER FAIRIES of the SUMMER

~ A ~ CELEBRATION

◆

CICELY MARY BARKER

FREDERICK WARNE

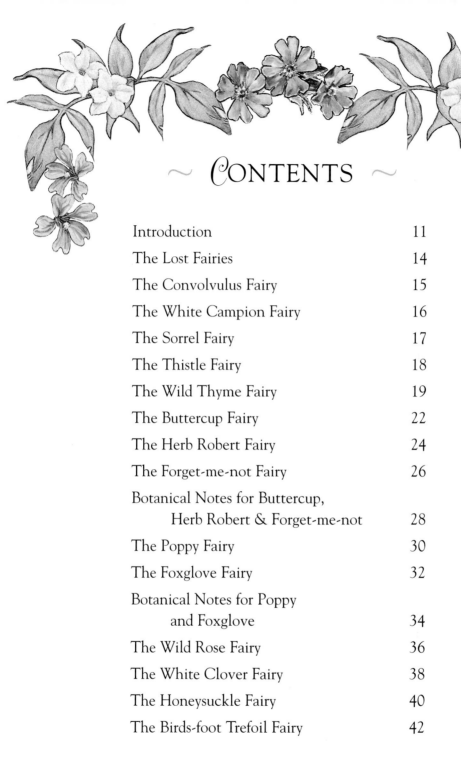

~ CONTENTS ~

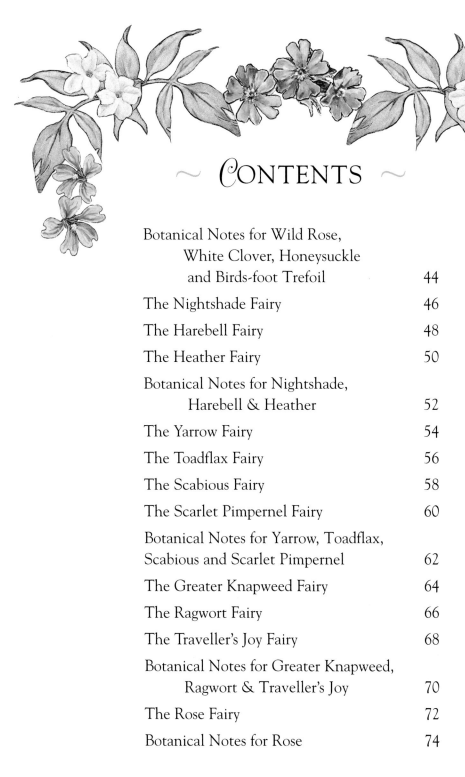

~ Contents ~

Spring Goes, Summer Comes

The little darling, Spring,
       Has run away;
The sunshine grew too hot for her to stay.

She kissed her sister, Summer,
       And she said:
"When I am gone, you must be queen
       instead."

Now reigns the Lady Summer,
       Round whose feet
A thousand fairies flock with blossoms sweet.

~ Introduction ~

Cicely Mary Barker was born in Croydon, South London, and lived there for most of her life, but her other home was in her imagination, and it is this magical fairy world that lives on in her poems and drawings. Although she was a modest, retiring person, she achieved commercial success and fame for her ever-popular Flower Fairies books. This volume celebrates the 75th anniversary of the publication of *Flower Fairies of the Summer*, the second in her celebrated series.

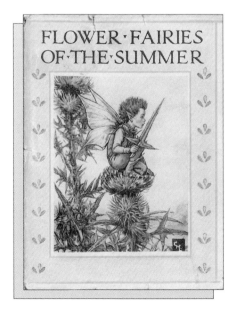 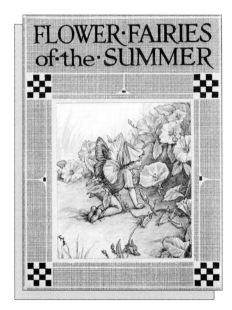

The jacket and cover from the first edition, printed in 1925.

Cicely Mary Barker was born on 28th June 1895. A frail child who suffered from epilepsy, Cicely was sheltered from the outside world by her parents and her older sister, Dorothy. The Barkers were deeply religious and Cicely herself was a devout Christian who used art to express her spiritual beliefs. Cicely's talent was evident from an early age. Her father was a capable watercolourist and he nurtured his daughter's talent for drawing, enrolling her at the Croydon Art Society when she was thirteen years old.

Cicely was only sixteen when she had her first work accepted for publication as a set of postcards and from that time she devoted her career to painting.

Between 1917 and 1918 Cicely embarked on the project that was to be her most famous. The Flower Fairies illustrations combined her two favourite subjects – children and nature – and her love of wildflowers and her minute attention to detail give her paintings a freshness and realism that is remarkable in the magical world of faerie. She was greatly influenced by the pre-raphaelites and believed, as they did, in 'truth to nature'. In creating her Flower Fairies books, she painted from life whenever she could, sometimes enlisting the help of staff at Kew gardens in finding and identifying plant specimens. She filled at least one sketchbook a year for all of her working life, leaving behind a rich collection of botanical drawings.

The sketches, many of which were drawn on her countryside holidays, are very detailed, allowing Cicely to concentrate on drawing her fairies from child models back in her studio. Cicely created the fairy costumes for the models to wear and fashioned miniature wings from twigs and gauze. The child models posed holding the flower they were representing, and when the paintings were complete Cicely wrote the accompanying poems. Sadly, few records exist of her preliminary sketches of local children, some of whom were pupils at her sister Dorothy's kindergarten.

Cicely produced a total of seven Flower Fairies books for her publisher Blackie, as well as two classic tales of her own, *The Lord of the Rushie River* and *Groundsel and Necklaces*. In addition to her children's illustrations, she painted many religious pictures. Cicely and her sister Dorothy were both Sunday school teachers and regular church-goers, and a collaboration between them produced a book of Bible stories entitled *He Leadeth Me*.

In 1954 Cicely's sister Dorothy died of a heart attack and Cicely took over reponsibility for looking after her elderly mother. This left little time for painting and her commercial career came to a halt. Nevertheless, Cicely remained the active vice-president of the Croydon Art Society between 1961 and 1972. On 16th February 1973, Cicely died at the age of 77. She is remembered for her kindness, her Christian faith and her prodigious artistic talent. Her spirit endures in the Flower Fairies, which continue to delight new generations of children.

~ The Lost Fairies ~

Flower Fairies of the Winter was compiled from the existing seven books in 1985. To create eight books of equal length, some of Cicely Mary Barker's original Flower Fairies were omitted from the new editions for editorial reasons, in some cases because the quality of the paintings had deteriorated. The following pages feature the five 'lost' fairies of *Flower Fairies of the Summer*.

The Convolvulus Fairy

The White Campion Fairy

The Sorrel Fairy

The Thistle Fairy

The Wild Thyme Fairy

19

Flower Fairies of the Summer

The Buttercup Fairy

~ The Song of ~
The Buttercup Fairy

'Tis I whom children love the best;
　　My wealth is all for them;
For them is set each glossy cup
　　Upon each sturdy stem.

O little playmates whom I love!
　　The sky is summer-blue,
And meadows full of buttercups
　　Are spread abroad for you.

~ The Song of ~
The Herb Robert Fairy

Little Herb Robert,
    Bright and small,
Peeps from the bank
    Or the old stone wall.

Little Herb Robert,
    His leaf turns red;
He's wild geranium,
    So it is said.

The Herb Robert Fairy

The Forget-me-not Fairy

~ The Song of ~
The Forget-me-not Fairy

So small, so blue, in grassy places
    My flowers raise
    Their tiny faces.

By streams my bigger sisters grow,
    And smile in gardens,
    In a row.

I've never seen a garden plot;
    But though I'm small
    Forget me not!

~ *Buttercup* ~
Ranunculus bulbosus

The Buttercup belongs to the Ranunculus family. There are three widespread native species of Buttercup: the bulbous Buttercup, the meadow Buttercup and the creeping Buttercup. All have flowers with five shiny yellow petals and five green sepals, differing mainly in their foliage and root systems. Although very pretty, and delightful as wayside flowers, Buttercups can be a nuisance in the garden where their growth can be invasive.

~ *Herb Robert* ~
Geranium robertianum

Herb Robert is part of the Geranium family, which includes the common wayside flowers known as Crane's-bill and Stork's-bill. All wild Geraniums have seed-pods with a long 'beak', which easily explains the bird references in the names.

As well as our native wild Geraniums, there are over a hundred species of perennial herbacious plants belonging to the same family. Hardy Geraniums tolerate most soil conditions but prefer good drainage. They will grow in both full sun and shade, depending on the variety.

~ Forget-me-not ~

Myosotis arvensis

The sky-blue flowers of the Forget-me-not are a welcome sight in early summer. They make good companion planting for tulips, as well as covering up the fading foliage of early crocuses and snowdrops. Forget-me-nots are easily grown from seed, either sown into nursery beds or scattered through the border. Once the foliage begins to fade the plants look untidy and can be removed, shaking the seed heads where desired in order to ensure new plants for the following year. Forget-me-nots can also have pink or white flowers, but blue is the traditional colour.

There are several stories in folklore about how the Forget-me-not got its name, but the most popular originated in Austria. Two young lovers were wandering along the banks of the Danube when the girl spotted a beautiful plant with tiny blue flowers floating down the river and said how sorry she was to see it being swept away. Her lover dived into the river and swam out to retrieve the flower, but as he made his way back he was sucked into a treacherous current and swept to his death. With the last of his strength he flung the flower into the hands of his lover and cried 'Vergiss mein nicht!': Forget me not.

The Poppy Fairy

~ The Song of ~ The Poppy Fairy

The green wheat's a-growing,
    The lark sings on high;
In scarlet silk a-glowing,
    Here stand I.

The wheat's turning yellow,
    Ripening for sheaves;
I hear the little fellow
    Who scares the bird-thieves.

Now the harvest's ended,
    The wheat-field is bare;
But still, red and splendid,
    I am there.

~ The Song of ~
The Foxglove Fairy

"Foxglove, Foxglove,
　　What do you see?"
The cool green woodland,
　　The fat velvet bee;
Hey, Mr Bumble,
　　I've honey here for thee!

"Foxglove, Foxglove,
　　What see you now?"
The soft summer moonlight
　　On bracken, grass, and bough;
And all the fairies dancing
　　As only they know how.

The Foxglove Fairy

～ Poppy ～

Papaver rhoeas

Poppies are some of the most beautiful of our native plants. Once commonly seen in cornfields, modern farming methods have reduced their numbers dramatically, although they can still be found in pockets along field margins and by the wayside. The elegantly branched, bristly stems bear magnificent scarlet flowers, up to eight centimetres across. The black stamens provide a wonderful contrast with the petals.

The Poppy has come to symbolise remembrance this century, being strongly identified with the fallen of two world wars. Every year many people wear a Poppy in their button-hole on Remembrance Sunday and give donations to charities supporting the veterans of war.

The Papaver family includes the well-loved garden flower, the oriental Poppy. A brilliantly coloured perennial, native to Asia Minor, it can grow as high as three or four feet. Originally orange-scarlet, with a deep purple base, the flowers are now also available in salmon-pink, bright crimson and white. These plants will grow in any good deep garden soil, but prefer to be left undisturbed. Most require staking.

All native Poppies contain a narcotic substance in their stems, and the opium Poppy is named for its derivative. The opium made from these Poppies was a great boon to medicine by helping to relieve pain as far back as the Middle Ages.

~ Foxglove ~

Digitalis purpurea

There are two theories to explain whence the Foxglove derived its name. The first claims that Foxglove is a corruption of 'little-folk's gloves' because the fairies wear its flowers as gloves or hats. However, some people believe that the flower earned its name because sly foxes used its blossoms as gloves to muffle their tread when out stealing chickens! Whichever derivation you prefer, Foxglove is a much nicer name than this fairy flower's other names – Goblin's Gloves, Witches' Thimbles and even Dead Man's Fingers.

It is possible that the Foxglove was given these other, sinister names because it is poisonous. It contains digitalis, a chemical that has proved remarkably helpful in stabilising heart conditions, but which can be fatal if taken in too great a quantity.

The wild Foxglove hardly differs from its garden cousins. Both are biennial, flowering in the second year of growth, and both prefer a sheltered location, either in sun or semi-shade. The wild Foxglove's distinctive purple blossoms are often seen in open woodland. Another foxglove, *Digitalis Lutea*, native to France and Belgium but now naturalised in chalky areas in Britain, is yellow. The choice of colours for the garden now extends to apricot, white and different shades of pink and purple. Whatever the colour, the Foxglove's stately spires add height and grace to the summer border.

The Wild Rose Fairy

36

~ The Song of ~
The Wild Rose Fairy

I am the queen whom everybody knows:
 I am the English Rose;
As light and free as any Jenny Wren,
 As dear to Englishmen;
As joyous as a Robin Redbreast's tune,
 I scent the air of June;
My buds are rosy as a baby's cheek;
 I have one word to speak,
One word which is my secret and my song,
'Tis "England, England, England" all day long.

~ The Song of ~
The White Clover Fairy

I'm little White Clover, kind and clean;
Look at my threefold leaves so green;
Hark to the buzzing of hungry bees:
"Give us your honey, Clover, please!"

Yes, little bees, and welcome, too!
My honey is good, and meant for you!

The White Clover Fairy

The Honeysuckle Fairy

~ The Song of ~
The Honeysuckle Fairy

The lane is deep, the bank is steep,
　　The tangled hedge is high;
And clinging, twisting, up I creep,
　　And climb towards the sky.
O Honeysuckle, mounting high!
O Woodbine, climbing to the sky!

The people in the lane below
　　Look up and see me there,
Where I my honey-trumpets blow,
　　Whose sweetness fills the air.
O Honeysuckle, waving there!
O Woodbine, scenting all the air!

41

~ The Song of ~
The Birds-foot Trefoil Fairy

Here I dance in a dress like flames,
And laugh to think of my comical names.
Hoppetty hop, with nimble legs!
Some folks call me *Bacon and Eggs*!
While other people, it's really true,
Tell me I'm *Cuckoo's Stockings* too!
Over the hill I skip and prance;
I'm *Lady's Slipper,* and so I dance,
Not like a lady, grand and proud,
But to the grasshoppers' chirping loud.
My pods are shaped like a dicky's toes:
That is what *Bird's-Foot Trefoil* shows;
This is my name which grown-ups use,
But children may call me what they choose.

The Birds-foot Trefoil Fairy

~ Wild Rose ~

Rosa rubiginosa

The Sweet Briar is native to Britain and one of the flowers most loved by poets. The Rose is a shrub with strong, arching stems, up to 1.5 metres tall, with apple-scented leaves. The flowers are pink with numerous yellow stamens, covering the shrub in profusion in early summer.

Once the petals have fallen the hips turn red and give a continued show into the autumn. In earlier times the hips would be collected and made into rose-hip syrup and rose-water.

~ White Clover ~

Trifolium repens

White Clover is one of the most important fodder plants and is frequently sown in pastures and in hay meadows. As Cicely's rhyme indicates, it is also loved by bees and gives a sweet, aromatic flavour to honey. It is a lovely treat for domestic pets such as rabbits and guinea-pigs.

Although an unwelcome intruder on a well-kept lawn, Clover is an easily recognisable and widespread wayside plant.

~ Honeysuckle ~

Lonicera periclymenum

Honeysuckle, or Woodbine, is a favourite wayside and garden plant. Its yellow or purple flowers are sweetly-scented and scramble happily through hedges and over trellises. The flowers are followed by small red or purple berries which stay on the plant into the winter.

Popular garden Honeysuckles include the Winter Honeysuckle, *Lonicera x purpusii*. Vigorous, and with a spreading habit, it is mainly grown for its small, sweetly fragrant white flowers.

~ Birds-foot Trefoil ~

Lotus corniculatus

This little yellow flower has a host of different names. Its most common name, Bird's-foot Trefoil, refers to the elongated seed pods that spread stiffly out from the stalk like the toes of a sparrow from its leg. The buds are deep red and flattened, vaguely resembling rashers of bacon. As they are mixed with the egg-yolk coloured open flowers, this explains the particularly curious nickname, Bacon and Eggs!

Bird's-foot Trefoil is widespread in Britain but is often partially hidden amongst taller grasses.

The Nightshade Fairy

~ The Song of ~
The Nightshade Fairy

My name is Nightshade, also Bittersweet;
    Ah, little folk, be wise!
Hide you your hands behind you when we meet,
    Turn you away your eyes.
My flowers you shall not pick, nor berries eat,
    For in them poison lies.

(Though this is so poisonous, it is not the
Deadly Nightshade, but the Woody Nightshade.
The berries turn red a little later on.)

~ The Song of ~ The Harebell Fairy

O bells, on stems so thin and fine!
    No human ear
    Your sound can hear,
O lightly chiming bells of mine!

When dim and dewy twilight falls,
    Then comes the time
    When harebells chime
For fairy feasts and fairy balls.

They tinkle while the fairies play,
    With dance and song,
    The whole night long,
Till daybreak wakens, cold and grey,
And elfin music fades away.

(The Harebell is the Bluebell of Scotland.)

The Harebell Fairy

The Heather Fairy

~ THE SONG of ~ THE HEATHER FAIRY

"Ho, Heather, ho! From south to north
Spread now your royal purple forth!
Ho, jolly one! From east to west,
The moorland waiteth to be dressed!"

I come, I come! With footsteps sure
I run to clothe the waiting moor;
From heath to heath I leap and stride
To fling my bounty far and wide.

(The Heather in the picture is Bell Heather,
or Heath; it is different from the common
Heather which is also called Ling.)

~ Nightshade ~

Solanum dulcamara

The poisonous Woody Nightshade or Bittersweet is part of the Solanum, or Potato family.

The flowers are very attractive and scramble over small trees and shrubs. Woody Nightshade has purple petals that turn back on themselves to reveal the yellow anthers protruding in a yellow cone. After flowering the plant bears red berries.

Closely related to the Woody Nightshade is the Black Nightshade whose globular black berries give it its name.

Perhaps the best known of the Nightshade family is the Deadly Nightshade. This plant looks very different from its namesakes, being a stout, shrubby-looking plant with long drooping bell-shaped flowers of brown-ish purple or green. These are followed by glossy black berries. The whole plant is very poisonous and should not be touched.

Two striking garden plants belong to the Potato family: *Solanum crispum* and *Solanum jasminoides*. The former is a vigorous scrambling shrub that can be evergreen in warmer areas. Loose clusters of purple and yellow star-shaped flowers appear over a long period in summer. The stems need tying to a support. *Solanum jasminoides* is similar in appearance but is of a climbing habit. Semi-evergreen and slender-stemmed, it will grow vigorously through shrubs and over trellises. The purple and yellow flowers appear from early summer to autumn. There is also a delightful white form. All these plants need a sunny position to thrive and benefit from protection during the winter.

~ Harebell ~

Campanula rotundifolia

Although the Harebell is known as the Bluebell in Scotland, the two plants are unrelated. The Harebell is part of the Campanula or Bellflower family, and is a perennial plant that flowers in midsummer. The English Bluebell is a bulb that flowers in late spring. Superfically though, they look quite similar, with their delicate sky-blue drooping flowers and hairless stems. Cicely Mary Barker included the Bluebell fairy in *Flower Fairies of the Spring*.

~ Heather ~

Ranunculus bulbosus

All Heathers belong to the Erica family and require open situations and acid soil in which to thrive. They are widespread in Britain and dominant on heath and moorland, open woods and around bogs.

In the garden, Heathers are very popular for underplanting Rhododendrons and other lime-hating shrubs. The many different varieties offer different shades of red, purple, pink and white, and a careful selection of Heathers can guarantee blossoms in the garden all year round.

~ The Song of ~
The Yarrow Fairy

Among the harebells and the grass,
   The grass all feathery with seed,
I dream, and see the people pass:
   They pay me little heed.

And yet the children (so I think)
   In spite of other flowers more dear,
Would miss my clusters white and pink,
   If I should disappear.

(The Yarrow has another name, Milfoil,
which means Thousand Leaf; because her leaves
are all made up of very many tiny little leaves.)

The Yarrow Fairy

The Toadflax Fairy

~ The Song of ~
The Toadflax Fairy

The children, the children,
    they call me funny names,
They take me for their darling
    and partner in their games;
They pinch my flowers' yellow mouths,
    to open them and close,
Saying, *Snap-Dragon!*
    Toadflax!
      or, *darling Bunny-Nose!*

The Toadflax, the Toadflax,
    with lemon-coloured spikes,
With funny friendly faces
    that everybody likes,
Upon the grassy hillside
    and hedgerow bank it grows,
And it's *Snap-Dragon !*
    Toadflax!
      and *darling Bunny-Nose!*

~ THE SONG of ~
THE SCABIOUS FAIRY

Like frilly cushions full of pins
For tiny dames and fairykins;

Or else like dancers decked with gems,
My flowers sway on slender stems.

They curtsey in the meadow grass,
And nod to butterflies who pass.

The Scabious Fairy

The Scarlet Pimpernel Fairy

~ The Song of ~
The Scarlet Pimpernel Fairy

By the furrowed fields I lie,
Calling to the passers-by:
"If the weather you would tell,
Look at Scarlet Pimpernel."

When the day is warm and fine,
I unfold these flowers of mine;
Ah, but you must look for rain
When I shut them up again!

Weather-glasses on the walls
Hang in wealthy people's halls:
Though I lie where cart-wheels pass
I'm the Poor Man's Weather-Glass!

~ *Yarrow* ~

Achillea millefolium

This strongly-scented, feathery-leaved plant is very common along the wayside and in open grassland. It is of an upright habit and has clusters of tiny creamy-white flowers bunched together into flat flower-heads.

Yarrow's garden relatives resemble their common cousin quite closely. Achillea 'Coronation Gold' and 'Gold Plate' are striking, long-flowering perennials that flourish happily in dry, stony soil. The sturdy stems do not require staking, and the plants will grow into thick clumps if left undisturbed.

~ *Toadflax* ~

Linaria vulgaris

The common Toadflax is a perennial plant with flowers like tiny yellow snapdragons, but with long spurs hanging from the lower lip. These contain nectar, and Toadflax is popular with bees. The unusual shape and bright yellow colour make it an attractive flower, and it is commonly found throughout most of Britain.

Its garden cousin, the Snapdragon (*Antirrhinum*), a popular summer annual bedding plant, shares the Toadflax's endearing ability to open and close its mouth if squeezed gently just at the point where the 'lips' join.

~ Scabious ~

Knautia arvensis

The field Scabious is common in pastures, on downlands and scrub, tolerating dry conditions and a chalky soil. It is a perennial with strong hairy stems, bearing flat-topped blue flowerheads on long stalks.

Scabious is a popular garden plant, preferring a good well-drained soil and flowering from June to October. *Scabiosa caucasica*, from the Caucasus, is perhaps the finest of the perennial species, reaching 90 centimetres in height. It has lavender-blue flowers up to 10 centimetres across.

~ Scarlet Pimpernel ~

Anagallis arvensis

This annual plant can easily be overlooked because of its prostrate, creeping habit. The plant is still common in cornfields and along the wayside despite the widespread use of modern herbicides. It is probably native to sand dunes and prefers sandy or chalky soil. The flowers are salmon-red rather than scarlet, and are borne singly on long stalks.

Cicely Mary Barker's rhyme discloses the Scarlet Pimpernel's useful habit of closing its flowers when rain is approaching.

~ The Song of ~
The Greater Knapweed Fairy

Oh, please, little children, take note of my
    name:
To call me a thistle is really a shame:
I'm harmless old Knapweed, who grows
    on the chalk,
I never will prick you when out for your
    walk.

Yet I should be sorry, yes, sorry indeed,
To cut your small fingers and cause them
    to bleed;
So bid me Good Morning when out for
    your walk,
And mind how you pull at my very tough
    stalk.

(Sometimes this Knapweed is called Hardhead;
and he has a brother, the little Knapweed, whose
flower is not quite like this.)

64

The Greater Knapweed Fairy

The Ragwort Fairy

~ The Song of ~
The Ragwort Fairy

Now is the prime of Summer past,
    Farewell she soon must say;
But yet my gold you may behold
    By every grassy way.

And what though Autumn comes apace,
    And brings a shorter day?
Still stand I here, your eyes to cheer,
    In gallant gold array.

~ The Song of ~
The Traveller's Joy Fairy

Traveller, traveller, tramping by
To the seaport town where the big ships lie,
See, I have built a shady bower
To shelter you from the sun or shower.
Rest for a bit, then on, my boy!
Luck go with you, and Traveller's Joy!

Traveller, traveller, tramping home
From foreign places beyond the foam,
See, I have hung out a white festoon
To greet the lad with the dusty shoon.
Somewhere a lass looks out for a boy:
Luck be with you, and Traveller's Joy!

(Traveller's Joy is Wild Clematis; and when the
flowers are over, it becomes a mass of silky fluff,
and then we call it Old-Man's-Beard.)

The Traveller's Joy Fairy

～ Greater Knapweed ～

Centaurea Scabiosa

The Greater Knapweed is common on chalk soils and lime grasslands in southern parts of Britain. The flowerheads are striking and showy, up to 5 centimetres wide, and flower in mid-summer.

The garden relative that most resembles the Knapweed is the perennial Cornflower (*Centaurea montana*). This long-standing garden favourite forms leafy clumps and produces large heads of blue flowers in early summer. It requires little care, is fully hardy, and will thrive in a sunny position.

～ Ragwort ～

Senecio jacobaea

This bright, sunny plant is common throughout Britain on roadsides, wasteland and in neglected pastures. It is a sturdy, erect perennial (sometimes biennial), that can reach a height of 1 metre. The flowers are bright yellow, with a daisy-like shape, and appear from mid-summer into autumn. Despite its cheerful appearance, Ragwort is poisonous to livestock, particularly horses, and should be removed from pasture before allowing animals to graze.

~ Traveller's Joy ~

Ranunculus bulbosus

The wild Clematis is a woody climbing shrub that scrambles happily through small trees, shrubs and hedges, giving all-year interest. As the rhyme indicates, the pretty, fragrant, creamy flowers give it the name of 'Traveller's Joy' in summer, while the feathery clusters of seed-heads, which give the appearance of clumps of fine hair on wood borders or hedges in autumn, are an obvious reason for its other name, 'Old Man's Beard'.

The flowers are freely borne in July and August, and are a familiar sight in chalk and limestone districts.

There are many different types of Clematis for gardens, enough to give all-year colour if planted with care. *Clematis montana* is a vigorous climber producing blankets of leafy growth and reaching up to 10 metres. The large spring flowers are borne in abundance and come in shades of white and pink, depending upon the named variety. It will grow happily in sun and partial shade.

The most popular Clematis varieties are the large-flowered hybrids. They come in almost all colours and are suitable both for training against a wall and for scrambling over large shrubs, seldom reaching a height of more than 3 metres.

The Rose Fairy

~ The Song of ~
The Rose Fairy

Best and dearest flower that grows,
Perfect both to see and smell;
Words can never, never tell
Half the beauty of a Rose—
Buds that open to disclose
Fold on fold of purest white,
Lovely pink, or red that glows
Deep, sweet-scented. What delight
    To be Fairy of the Rose!

~ *R*ose ~

Rosa

The Rose is probably the single best-loved garden plant, famed not only for its beauty but also for its delicate fragrance. The red Rose has traditionally been associated with love and passion, and is now the most popular gift on Valentine's day. The white Rose is chiefly associated with purity: the two flowers most commonly symbolising the Virgin Mary are the Lily and the Rose.

The Rose also has an important place in British history. The famous Wars of the Roses were so named because the House of Lancaster's emblem was the red Rose; the House of York's emblem was the white. Henry VII (a Lancastrian) finally united the two houses by marrying Elizabeth of York and created a new emblem for the House of Tudor; the red and white Tudor Rose.

As befits the Rose's popularity, a Rose can be found for nearly every garden, from the useful ground cover Rose to the vigorous ramblers that can reach 10 metres in both height and spread. Roses have also been bred to have several different flower shapes, from the old 'cabbage' Rose to the pointed elegance of the hybrid Teas.

These Roses are some of the most popular of the different categories:

'Mme Isaac Pereire' (large shrub Rose)
A lovely bourbon Rose with vigorous, arching branches and richly fragrant flowers of a deep pink with magenta shading. It appears from summer into autumn and can attain a height of over 2 metres.

'Rosa Mundi' (small shrub Rose)
This well-known Rose was beloved in medieval times. It has double flowers of a pale pink with crimson stripes and will grow to 1 metre height and spread.

'Maigold' (climbing Rose)
A vigorous climber with thorny stems and lush foliage. Fragrant yellow blooms appear in early summer and, less profusely, in the autumn. It will achieve a height and spread of 4 metres.

'Albertine' (rambler)
An old and popular rambling Rose with richly fragrant, double salmon-pink flowers, freely borne in summer on vigorous growth of up to 5 metres height and spread. Although only once-flowering, the sheer profusion of colour and scent makes it a classic cottage garden Rose.

'Peace' (hybrid tea)
First launched in 1945, hence its name, this pinky-yellow Rose is a classic hybrid Tea. It has a good fragrance, strong growth and flowers from mid-summer to autumn.

The reproductions in this book have been made using the most modern electronic scanning methods from entirely new transparencies of Cicely mary Barker's original watercolours. They enable Cicely Mary Barker's skill as an artist to be appreciated as never before.

FREDERICK WARNE

Published by the Penguin Group
27 Wrights Lane, London W8 5TZ, England
Penguin Putnam Inc., 375 Hudson Street, New York, New York 10014, USA
Penguin Books Canada Ltd, 10 Alcorn Avenue, Toronto, Ontario, Canada M4V 3BN
Penguin Books (NZ) Ltd, 182-190 Wairau Road, Auckland 10, New Zealand
Penguin Books India (P) Ltd, 11, Community Centre, Panchsheel Park, New Delhi 110 017, India
Penguin Books (South Africa) (pty) Ltd, 5 Watkins Street, Denver Ext 4, 2094, South Africa
Penguin Books Ltd, Registered Offices: Harmondsworth, Middlesex, England

First published in 2000

1 3 5 7 9 10 8 6 4 2

ISBN 0 7232 4628 9

Colour reproduction by Saxon Photolitho Ltd, Norwich
Printed and bound in Singapore by Imago Publishing Ltd.